TABLE OF CONTENTS

Chapter 1: Truth or Dare

Chapter 2: There's Nothing in the Back

Chapter 3: Cash Cooper

Chapter 4: Game Plan

Chapter 5: "Is she even missing?"

Chapter 6: "Where is she?"

Chapter 7: Mom's "Friends"

Chapter 8: Little Victories

Chapter 9: Connect my Dead Mother to my Living Father

Chapter 10: Ask and You Shall Receive..

Chapter 11: Chicken and Half Truths. 25

Chapter 12: The Truth

Chapter 13: He Wins and Loses

Chapter 14: News

Maybe I imagined It
By Jamie Weaver

CHAPTER 1: TRUTH OR DARE

One of my earliest memories is my father waking me in the middle of the night to help him bury my mother. I got up without a sound. I never asked questions, he wouldn't respond anyway. I don't know how but I knew my mother was dead in the back of my dad's car. I didn't even see her; I only saw a form in the sleeping bag she normally slept in. The shovel was thrown on top.
I never sat in the front seat until that night. I was seven or eight and I've never breathed a word of it until at 20 years old, I had my first sleepover with my best friend Rae.

Without my best friend, I would have died. Don't think I mean this figuratively, I know Rae saved my life. She fed me, lifted me up and eventually took me in. She and I met when we were twelve and she felt sorry for me. She swears she didn't, but of course she did. I was the poor kid, the smelly kid, the one who's dad loved beer more than his own child. My "Rae of Sunshine" took me to church and would sneak food into my book bag to take home for dinner. Eventually, I became so close with their family that Rae's parents asked me to move in. Since my dad was still collecting government checks for me, I thought he was going to offer to pack a bag for me. The only thing that I left of my sad existence in that old trailer was a red sleeping bag whose twin bag held my mother's corpse years ago.

My father was a walking contradiction - a drinking man who hated the government but depended on them to "feed" his hungry kid. He hated any authority figures, especially the police. He called them "worthless thieves and liars" but yet he would become enraged when they wouldn't do their job by giving someone else a speeding ticket. My father hated people knowing his business and he despised anyone who told him his way was wrong. If our neighbor's house was dirty or the front porch had garbage, he would call them "worthless trailer park trash."

To appreciate the irony, you would only have to spend one day as a roach on our kitchen counter. He did things his way and there was no arguing with him.

This is the part where you're expecting I tell you about my mother, the saint. Not this story. Real life isn't that way. Most of the time, drunks end up with other drunks. Angry, bitter, druggies usually have angry hate-filled drunken sex with other miserable people, who, just because they accidentally get pregnant and keep the child-poof!- become (What's the word again, Ariel?) Oh, parents.

My mother was an angry drug addict who, if you believe my father, was a whore who had sex for drugs and money. She slept on his couch while she was pregnant and although my father (in his words) "only did it with her that one time" actually believed her baby could be his and he was "sure wasn't gonna let no pimp have his kid." Although I have never heard that my mom had a pimp, the stories about her are no less damaging. Stories I only heard from her "friends" when I was 20 after I walked into that police station with a horrific story told through the eyes of a scared seven year old kid.

It was the night after I had my first sleepover with friends. Yup, at 20 years old! My dad never let me go anywhere while I was living with him and of course I didn't dare have friends over to my nasty house. When I was 16, I finally got a job and over the course of a year was able to move my things to Rae's. I had her brother's old room and I guess we got too old to have sleepovers.

I don't know why it didn't come up before or even how it came up when we were attending college but Rae said something about "you know, when you're having a sleepover and if you fall asleep first, your friends get to put make up on you!"

I looked at her sideways and she almost started to cry. She knew how bad it was and we didn't talk about my "life with father" much so it was a little surprising for her to know, that on top of the hunger, neglect, ridicule and belittling…I never had a sleepover.

It was almost as if my death of childhood resurrected Rae because she was glowing. She was making plans and calling friends, begging me to share her excitement.

One of the most annoying things about me, Rae says very sadly, is my inability to get excited about anything. I hardly ever smile and when I do, it's never a full smile. Rae always says to me "smile with teeth, Stacey". She always said I have the prettiest smile when I show my teeth. I expect and almost always receive disappointment. It's from years of being lied to by a man who, if he could muster a smile, would only come from his daughter's anticipation of something good that he would go to the ends of the Earth to ruin.

He would deliberately say I could go to a carnival…oh…why do I lie? Let's be honest, even as a child, I was smart enough to know my father would never let me go to a carnival. I wasn't allowed to have a few dollars to take to school when we had a bake sale or a book fair. I wasn't allowed to have a bike, much less ride one. My father mastered the art of blaming me, age 8, of not having a job and then not letting me, age 8, walk our neighbors dog for $2. He was in control at all times and if I even thought I would enjoy a brief moment of reprieve from my undeserved prison, the door would be slammed shut and he would tell me it was my fault.

One time I got some cash. Here's where you'll see the mind games my father loved to play. I lied to my neighbor, Ms. Candy, and told her my dad allowed me to walk her dog and clean up all the poop for $5. You know how you're supposed to clean up poop in your yard? Well, she didn't.

I swear I worked forever, making sure my dad didn't see me outside. I got the fiver and sneaked it into my lunch bag. I was, dare I say, excited? I got up so early to catch the bus - I was waiting by my front door, in the dark for over an hour, secretly hiding my money between my sandwich and frozen juice box. I was so overjoyed to be able to buy something at school but of course, in my haste to conceal my earnings; my frozen juice box had melted through the paper bag. When I saw the bus rounding the corner, I ran out the door, my juice box, sandwich and money flying behind me.

My father picked up the cash, looked at me with sheer disgust and quietly said "you worthless thief" and put it in his pocket.

If the bus hadn't been slap full of witnesses, I don't know what would have happened. Although my father reined over our kingdom with fear, yelling and always getting the final, and sometimes only, word he never laid a hand on me. I think it's because he used to brag that "I've never laid a

hand on you".
Even sociopaths have their honor.

Sorry! Since I spilled my secret, I feel like I can't stop talking! I held back so much growing up that when that dam broke, it just hasn't stopped.
Back to Rae and the sleepover that changed so many lives.
Rae had big ideas for the party. She swore she would do everything for me that I never got to do. Girls reading this know that whoever falls asleep first is just asking for a makeover or a hand in cold water.
I won't bore you (You- who had probably 20 sleepovers) with the details of my first sleepover with my first real friends but it was the greatest ever! "Prank" calls to stores, fish-tail braiding my long dark hair and eating everything in sight. It was literally all fun and games until truth or dare. I was asked "truth or dare, Stacey?"
Deciding to step out of my comfort zone around these 5 friends I said "truth".
One of the girls then asked me something that stopped my heart. "Tell us a secret you've never told anyone, not even Rae."
What seemed like hours, all I could do was look at Rae and softly shook my head "no". Since everyone was staring at me. Once again, my "Rae of sunshine" saved the day.
She didn't know what the look meant but only my ride-or-die friend knew that I just couldn't speak. So Rae spoke for me.
"Guys! Don't let her get off easy! She needs to do a dare! A good one."
I ended up being dared to run out of the house in my sports bra and boy shorts to the mailbox and back. Easier than the truth. The girls eventually all fell asleep but I knew that the morning would shine light on my dark secret but it was

time to tell.

Although we went to college, Rae and I couldn't afford to stay in the dorms so our new college girl friends just spent the night at our house. They got up and left to go to the beach and Rae and I stayed home and promised to meet them later.

Rae was sitting on her bed waiting for me to spill my guts.

"Stacey", she said "You okay?"

That was Rae.

This was her lead in question in our entire relationship.

When I was sad.

Hungry.

Lonely.

"Stace, you okay?"

Then I would spill it.

Today was no different.

"My secret is ….I think my dad killed my mom"

We had to talk to Rae's mom. Mrs. Katherine was the best mother who gave amazing advice. I was welcomed in their Christian home and was loved and cared for from the very beginning. I hate to do this but I'm gonna write her name like I say it "Miss K" although she and Mr. James are still married, I've always said "Miss" but I wanted to be respectful because without them, I wouldn't know what parents were supposed to be like.

Its crazy the things you live that you become accustomed to. Things you think are normal but are so out of the ordinary. Like hunger.

My mom was a drug addict. Most addicts don't get hungry like non addicts so they just forget to eat. They forget to feed their kids.

I was always hungry. That was my normal.

Rae's mom listened to my secret. I explained that I didn't see or hear anything. I remember being shaken awake and it was dark.

I didn't ask anything, I knew not to.

We had 2 sleeping bags in our house and my mom always had one. It was red and warm on the inside and black shiny material outside. It was like her baby blanket.

Hmmm...funny the things you think as a child. At seven years old I thought of my mother as a child. She couldn't even take care of herself. She was selfish, would get mad and throw things and sometimes if she wanted to be with me, she would wake me up and move me over so she could hold me. Her breath always smelled of old beer or just neglect. I hated it. She didn't hold me when I needed holding, she held me when she wanted to be next to someone. She'd get drunk or high and talk nonsense to me, making me respond and shaking me awake until I agreed with whatever she was saying. Most of the time she asked me if I loved her and to tell her she was good. She didn't say she loved me. That's just like a kid, selfish and only thinking of themselves.

Again, the irony of shaking your exhausted, hungry kid until I said "yes, yes! I love you. You're a good mom. Please I've got school in the morning."

With all her uncertainties, her sleeping bag was her constant. She would take it with her when she got ticked at my father and would slam the door, with that sleeping bag always getting caught in the metal door to our trailer. It would rip the bottom and she never cut the snags and strings. She would leave with some random guy or skanky girl and then come back days later.

My mom had a sister somewhere but had long ago burnt

all the bridges with her family. I only knew this because it was part of my dad's little jabs while he was yelling at her. "Go ahead and leave! Where are you going, crack-head? Your parents don't want you back until you pay them all the money you stole! Going to Jenny's? Her husband said the next time he finds you on their porch; he's shooting you like the raccoons that dig in their trash. So go ahead and leave!"

Sorry - back to dad waking me up.
He had apparently already "loaded" the car.
"Get in the front."
I opened the door and looked back. My mom's sleeping bag was on the back seat with a figure in it. I knew it was my mom but in a court of law…I guess I didn't really know… but I knew..you know? So for this next part, I'll have to describe what I would think would be my mother's body as "the sleeping bag".
Funny.
I like weird stuff. Symbolism and puns are my thing. My mom, the bag. Dad's "old bag". My mom who slept a lot and "carried" me (like a bag) for 9 months. The "sleeping bag". I think it's funny. Sad, but funny.
We drove in the night.
I never really had been up at that time. There's something about being up at 3am (I'm just guessing since I didn't know the time).
It's black outside. I mean like BLACK. Like you were swallowed by a whale.
The night was only lit by the moon and my dad's headlights.
We drove a short while and pulled over on some gravel road. My dad got out and opened the back door on his side. He walked to my side and opened my door and handed me a shovel.

I got out and looked around.
I wasn't scared. I don't know what I was thinking.
My dad made a grunt as he lifted "the sleeping bag". He shut the door and walked towards the front of the car. He had "the sleeping bag" over his shoulder and I just followed him Holding the shovel.
We walked a little while until we got to some railroad tracks. Then we followed them down for a long time.
We didn't speak but that was normal.
We got to a spot and stopped, probably because my dad just couldn't go any farther. He had adjusted "the sleeping bag" so many times and he was pretty exhausted.
He put it down and took the shovel from me.
My dad, again, a walking contradiction. He hates people who do things lazy, "half-way" (his words are harsher) but sometimes my dad *is* that lazy guy. He probably dug on the side of those tracks for just ten minutes, cursing the rocks, the hard ground, God, and of course the life he was dealt. Never cursing himself for the choices he made just his terrible luck that he couldn't bury this bag easily.
Oh the irony.
He eventually gave up the hard way and decided he would take his chances on something easier. I remember him sliding, pulling and moving the bag under some brush while I tried to practice balancing on the train rail. I was the main attraction on the tight wire as I tried not to look down - not at my feet or down at my father's nefarious activities.
I don't know time or how far I played "tight rope" but he walked past me and I obediently followed him back to the car.
We got home like it was a trip to the grocery store and I went to bed without thinking at all.
I don't remember if I overslept and missed the bus, but it

wouldn't have been unusual.
The years went on and occasionally my mother's whereabouts would come up. My dad would say "she left with some guy. Never came back"
The thing about my dad is he's pretty smart. His lie was simple. That's all he said. That's all he ever had to say.
My mom had left before with some guy.
She was unreliable, unpredictable and frankly unpleasant. She "borrowed" money she never paid back, would just stay on someone's couch until she had to be removed and was a "user" in every definition of the word.
She was not a good daughter, sister, mother, or friend. Simply put; she was not missed. In fact, her departure was a relief.
So why did I care? So what if my feeling was right? My dad probably killed her and then buried her. So what?
She was my mom. I wanted to know. I guess in a way, I'm like my dad. Simple.
After hearing my story, Miss K said we no choice but to go to the police.

CHAPTER 2: THERE'S NOTHING IN THE BACK

We talked to a detective on duty who had a new rookie there with him. I felt so brave when I walked in and retold my story to them..
He was super patient but his first question hit me like a baseball bat in the head.
"So, we are in Georgia- you say this happened in South Carolina?"
Jurisdiction.
Crap.
Although we moved to Savannah, GA (which is only 30 or 45 minutes from South Carolina), it was out of his jurisdiction.
Second question he asked and another blow to my head:
"You don't know where she's buried?"
I couldn't even remember the name of the town I lived in at the time. We moved so much.
Third question and again, wham! Knocked me out.
"Was there a missing person file on her?"
Nope. She wasn't even missing.

And now the last question was the one that I had asked myself a thousand times.

"You think you remember him burying her, but you don't know if he killed her?"

Nope. He could have found her dead, maybe from a drug overdose or she could have killed herself? Maybe someone killed her? But why bury her if he didn't kill her? Without knowing what my dad knew, I had no answers for the detective.

His final statement was an offer of hope but we've all heard it before, like when you really wanted size 7 shoes but all they have are size 8s. "I'll check in the back"There was no back. No hope. You know there's nothing in the back, but you smile and say "thank you. I appreciate your help". I guess I had been wrong. This secret of epic proportions wasn't as big of a deal as I thought. Why did I lose sleep?

"I'll give you some phone numbers or I can call someone for you." he said.

Of course I said "thank you, I appreciate your help"

Crazy, right?

But when you think about it, how can I ask for help solving my mom's murder if she isn't even reported missing or I didn't know if it was even a murder.

He gave me some numbers and an address for a detective he knew in South Carolina. He told me he was real sorry that he couldn't do more but he had my statement and as soon as he wasn't busy, he would see what he could do.

He said I should keep him posted.

And I know that if Cash Cooper hadn't went with his gut and listened to that still small voice, that detective would have forgotten me the second I walked out the door.

CHAPTER 3: CASH COOPER

Rae, Miss K, and I were silently walking to our car which was parked about a block from the precinct downtown. I didn't know there was a man chasing me down until I heard him loudly exclaim "ma'am, your keys".

I didn't drive there so I didn't have my keys but there was the rookie cop who had been standing next to the detective holding some keys. "I'm a Bulldog fan too", he said, holding the GA Bull Dog keychain up and dangling the keys in the air.

"Oh, those aren't mine," I said. "And I'm not a bulldog fan, sorry"

"That's right", he said "You're from South Carolina. Clemson or Gamecock?"

I looked at him. It's a look I give to Rae. As much as I want to be the exact opposite of my father, it's *his* look and he owns it. If my father doesn't want to answer, talk, acknowledge or even admit that you are in his presence, he gives you this look.

Here, I'll teach you.

Think of a time that someone asked you something so personal, so incredible, so private that you were dumbfounded. It was none of their business. So you try and put your eyebrows close together, tighten your face, purse your lips and this is the kicker…you swallow.

Now take a breath. All while staring at them, not answering.

It's hard to do but if done right, that look makes the other person feel about two feet tall and hopefully go away like a scolded puppy. Its the look of "how dare you?"

I hate that I've done that to Rae and I hate that I'm doing it now but seriously, you're talking to me about sports? I just shared that my father buried my mother and there's nothing I can do about it.

A little embarrassed, he quickly introduced himself.

"I'm Cash Cooper", he said. "I think I could help you if you want."

I'm really good at letting people talk. So I kept staring. I swallowed again and cocked my head a little.

"So this is my first week on the force and I'm stuck on night shift. Today I was just hanging out before my shift began. I'm just so excited, I can't sleep and I really want to be a detective. I know I've got to work my way up and it can take years but investigating is in my blood. I don't have any experience but I know the law and I can help on my days off. Your story is intriguing. I can't be paid for this so I won't be in uniform so we don't need to worry about jurisdiction. I'm just a friend helping out. I can at least point you in the right direction."

My face softened. Rae's lit up and Miss K threw her arms around him.

"You're an answer to our prayers!", she squealed and jumped a little.

Again, you remember that I don't get too excited because I'm usually let down but in this "case", loving this pun, any help was better than what I could do on my own. I allowed myself to smile. Just a little. No teeth.

After we exchanged numbers and schedules, I found out that "Cash" was not his real name and thank the holy Trinity it wasn't short for "Cashmere" either. His name was Christian Cooper, named after his dad. His older sister couldn't say his name so she called him "Crash" after he began to walk and would fall down. They don't know how it changed but soon everyone called him Cash.

He loved lists and couldn't wait to call me to discuss our "strategy" and our "steps".
"Things have to go in order", he told me. "We need a game plan. Just like football. We need to know the competition. We need to know what they know and we need to be more prepared. We go in this with a list of what needs to be done and the questions that need answering. South Carolina isn't far but it's not down the street. We need to get as much done as we can while we are there."

CHAPTER 4: GAME PLAN

Step 1: "Is she even missing?"
Because all I saw was that sleeping bag with a figure and then I never saw my mom again, you know that's not grounds for anything but a simple investigation. For about 13 years, my mother has been "gone". We needed to find evidence that indicates that she is missing or dead. Maybe she really did leave with some guy and I dreamt that memory.

Maybe her body has been found but they didn't have a name to go with it. We need to look up unclaimed remains and see if any of them fit her profile. Where would I even find her dental records? Good grief.

Grief. I haven't felt that yet. Not sure if I ever have. You really have to love someone to have grief when they are gone and so far, no one I have loved has left me. Let that sink in.

Step 2: "Where is she?"
If she's missing, and presumed dead then where the heck is she buried?

We had to investigate where I went to school when I was 7 or 8 and try and find the address to my old home. Then we needed to find the closest train tracks, assuming that's where she is.

If she wasn't dead, then where has she been and where is she now? And on top of all the neglect I felt growing up, are you telling me that she's been alive this whole time and never once came to see me? She never cared about me then, maybe she doesn't now. How would I even start to look for her?

Step 3: "Connect my dead mother to my living father"
This is it. How do you get evidence or find an eyewitness or even hope for a confession? Even if they found her body and my father's DNA in that black and red sleeping bag after years of being in the elements, it still wouldn't prove anything. My father's DNA would be all over it. They both lived in that house. Maybe her body will tell us how she died but my father didn't do a great job of burying her so animals have long since scattered her remains.

Oh this is exhausting and we haven't even started! Cash was telling me his plan during one of our nightly phone calls. After I finished typing all the steps into my notes, I breathed heavily into my phone in the middle of Cash saying something about "Cold Case Prioritization" . He was explaining that my case actually ranked "high" because we had a suspect (my dad) and an eyewitness (me) but no known physical evidence.

He stopped when he heard me sigh again.

"It's too much" I said.

"So what else are you gonna do?"

Another simple answer man.

I took a breath and continued typing in my phone.

"How do you start a million mile journey?", Cash asked me. He answered quickly "with one step".

CHAPTER 5: "IS SHE EVEN MISSING?"

This step began around 1pm on a Tuesday. Our schedules did not match up very well, with me taking a full load of college courses and working for Ms. K plus with Cash having to work the night shift, this investigation could only be done maybe once a week when we both had a day off.

Cash insisted he pick me up and paid for gas while I saved money and made us some sandwiches. It was so weird for me to talk to a guy. I only had one friend and no guys ever noticed me. Although I'm 5'6 with long dark hair and petite, I was that stinky kid until I moved in permanently with Rae. She tried to teach me how to do my makeup and the one time I went to school with it on, I got a lot of attention. But it wasn't good. Girls and guys said mean things like "who are you trying to impress?" and "it looked like you put lipstick on a monkey". The next day, I hung my head and no one said anything. Back to being invisible, just like at home.

Cash started the conversation off really easily.

"Are you excited? I'm really excited. I feel like we can maybe solve a cold case."

"We don't even have a case." I said dryly.

"I know but we will be closer today than we were

yesterday."
"We just left my house. I don't want to get my hopes up"
"Stacey, you should be insanely proud of yourself. You shared a secret and even with the odds stacked against you, you are doing something. Right now, you are doing so much more than everyone who's ever wondered about a big decision. You are doing something about it. I'm really proud of you."

I smiled, lightly. No teeth. "Thanks".

We did a lot of prep work prior to just getting in the car and heading over the Talmadge bridge, I looked through old photos and yearbooks trying to find a date or location or school name when I was in 2nd grade. It turns out I went to Beaufort Elementary during that time so we called the school. It had been 13 years and they couldn't do anything over the phone. Since the school was closed on weekends, we had to go during school hours, during the week.
I remembered going to that elementary school vaguely. I went to the office with my I.D.
Cash was making calls outside while I went inside to ask if there were old records with my address on them. I couldn't remember where I lived and I was stammering trying to explain what I was doing there. I didn't think I would have to answer so many questions about my own records.
"You need to see your school records because you need your old address?" the receptionist at the front desk asked me, puzzled.
"Yes, I'm Stacey McClain and here's my birthday, I went here 13 years ago."
"We don't just give out records, you're going to need to fill this request form out. It may take 3-6 weeks. We will let you know."

I was used to never getting what I needed or wanted. My father did not allow back talk and I wasn't allowed to argue, ever. I always accepted defeat, usually before I was declared a loser. I simply didn't know how to protest or fight. At this point, you would think the next line would be "my eyes filled with tears".

Nope. My heart didn't sink, either.

People who have had hope understand their heart sinking but I didn't. See, I lived a life so full of hopelessness so that when someone says "no", I just accept it.

I took the paper and walked back to the car. Cash had finished his phone call and was excitedly telling me he had connected with the local police station and we could meet with them the next time we were in town.

"Okay, Stacey, all we need is your old address and I'll be able to meet with a local detective and make some progress."

"I need to fill out this form first." I said and then told him what happened. I had waited 13 years. I guess I could wait another 3 to 6 weeks.

He was outraged. "I really hoped it wouldn't come to this", he said and popped the trunk and pulled out a garment bag and put it in the back seat. "Hop in. I brought this just in case."

We drove to a local gas station, filled up and Cash went inside like Clark Kent and changed into his police uniform. We both went back into the school with a mission of purpose. Cash stood taller, walked faster and went in that office with me by his side. He took my ID right out of my hand and in a commanding tone said "We are in the middle of an investigation. This is Stacey McClain and she is requesting her public school records. If you aren't capable of producing them immediately, let me know who I need to speak with".

The woman who had so flippantly dismissed me quickly said
"Yes, sir. I was just waiting on her to fill out that form for me so I could have a formal request. I didn't know she had a court order"
No one said anything about a court order. And she called me "she", like I wasn't even there. Invisible. As always.
I took a breath and pursed my mouth and swallowed hard and said nothing. Cash spoke up.
"*She* is Stacey McClain. She gave you her valid identification and made a formal verbal request for *her* public school records that belong to *her*. We don't need a court order but if I do get one, I'm going to find out why you're making it so difficult for something so simple. I've been in this school for less than 3 minutes and I've already counted 2 violations. Number one, we are total strangers here and were not buzzed in per proper procedure, someone from inside opened the door. Two, (he pointed) you have a prescription medication bottle sitting behind that sign by the wall. Any child over 4 ft tall could take it and overdose. Now, I will assume that you became distracted and placed the bottle there while helping Ms. McClain obtain her records. I will also assume that as soon as you hand over those records, you will put that prescription bottle in a locked and secure location. We will wait while you do both."
I smiled huge and caught myself. I found it rather difficult to stop smiling so I hung my head down until my records could be found.
She went to a computer and asked my birthday and confirmed my name.
"Are 2 copies sufficient?" she asked me.
"Yes", I said. And with that, we were gone with what we

came for.

We didn't say anything about that awesome display of authority as we drove. I just looked over at him and laughed. He didn't even smile. "What?" he said all business. I laughed so hard I snorted and then laughed even harder. Cash started to laugh and shook his head. We didn't talk about it, we just laughed.

It was interesting looking through my records. I found my old address and asked Cash if I could put it in his phone to see how far away we were. Ugh. We were 28 minutes away from it in the opposite direction from the way we came.

I sighed again. Did I really ride the school bus for 28 minutes twice a day?

"I thought we could visit your old house if you wanted?" Cash asked me.

"Oh, It's kind of far, we can just go back to Savannah"

"It's not that far, maybe something might ring a bell?"

"I guess but it's an hour round trip"

"Stacey, don't forget why we are here. This is our only day to do this, let's make the most of our time."

That was me, making sure I didn't cause more work or "headache" like my dad said.

We arrived at that run down trailer that I had called home and where my mother had died. It had long been abandoned. We were just renting it when we lived there. It was over grown, dirty and the porch was rickety and there was a bucket next to the door to hold cigarettes. It was almost exactly as I remembered it.

We pulled on the door but it didn't open. Cash went around to every door and window, trying to get something to open or see inside .I felt like Cash always just went the extra mile. He wanted evidence and he was treating this old trailer like a crime scene. But it had been 13 years. I'm sure other

renters had lived in this place and made their own horrible memories. Some places just breathe grief. After helping my father bury my dead mother, we moved shortly after to another crappy trailer and then another and another. Dad stayed in South Carolina and I moved in with Rae when I was 17. Her family moved to Savannah and now you are up to date.
Cash tried to open the last window and gave up.

I made Cash stop at another gas station because I had to grab a Cheerwine soda and peanuts. "What are you doing?" Cash looked at me as I poured the peanuts into the bottle of Cheerwine.
"It's a thing", I said.
"Let me try it", he said so I took his Pepsi and poured my remaining salted peanuts carefully into the long neck bottle. Cash took a swig.
 "I don't get it ".
"It's best when its at the end and you eat the peanuts", I reminisced. "My dad taught me."
Cue nostalgic music and an image of a little me in the back seat sobbing over another rough day. I hated school. You know why.
"Here, stop crying," my dad handed me his Cheerwine filled with nuts. "Try and drink it until you get to the peanuts".
After I shared that story with Cash, he took a big gulp and said
"So, that's something nice from your childhood that you held onto."
"Yeah, I'm sure he wanted me to shut up and this was the fastest way of doing it ."
But Cash was right, it had been so long since I had a good memory of my father, I pretended that him sharing this drink with me was my dad being kind and maybe he liked

me.

I made a discovery right then. I realized that whenever I was feeling low, I had a Cheerwine with nuts. It always cheered me up, no pun intended. Hmmm.

Drinking this childhood soda and driving in my old neighborhood made me want to open up a little.

"So," I said, "I know I'm weird and this will just add to it. But whenever I picture myself as a child, okay this is hard to explain but I picture me now -the adult me - holding my own hand as a child. I never remember just me doing something , the adult me is always there too. Or sometimes *Adult Stacey* is sitting on the bed watching *Kid Stacey* try and wake up *our* passed out mom so we could have our bed back. Like when I think about the night dad took me on the train tracks to bury my mom, my adult self is there walking next to kid Stacey trying to balance on the rails in the dark."

"Makes perfect sense to me." Cash said.

"Okay, Sigmund, enlighten me."

"Stacey, you were never protected. Not by your mom or dad or the police when you were a child. So who knows child Stacey better than adult Stacey? You wish you could've been there for her during her darkest times. So it makes sense that you're there for her in your memories."

"I think you saved me a year in therapy."

He kind of chuckled. "You're smart, Stace, you would have figured it out."

CHAPTER 6: "WHERE IS SHE?"

Another 2 weeks went by before we could get a day off together but we talked on the phone at least once a day. I was eager to listen to Cash and his stories about his nighttime police route. He would say that he couldn't believe the amount of people in downtown Savannah that seemed to start their day around 6pm and drink with their friends until 2a.m. By that time they were highly intoxicated and that's when the fights started and he had to respond.

He genuinely liked hearing about how my sophomore year of college was starting out and was concerned when I began to doubt my major as a computer engineer. I always wanted to stay behind the scenes so I thought I would like being behind a computer screen, but I hated it. Algorithms, math, science, it didn't matter; I was lost in it all.

Cash would only let me complain so much before asking me the daunting question Rae had asked me so many times, the same one I asked myself every time I sat in front of that screen. "Why do you want to be a computer engineer?"

I told him that I heard they make good money, I liked being invisible and I never wanted to be hungry or poor ever again. I am paraphrasing because I think I told him about ten stories of my childhood poverty before he said "okay, you want to be rich, but why computer engineering?" When I said I didn't know, he suggested I should meet with someone who can help me answer that question I took his advice went to the guidance counselor.

Cash and I talked a lot about the investigation and this time we discussed going to my mom's old stomping grounds to see if anyone saw or heard from her after that night on the tracks, whenever that was. I had to make sure I didn't imagine it. My dad told anyone who would ask that she left with some guy and slowly that memory of the night on the tracks merged with dreams and nightmares. A few months after that night, I couldn't tell them apart. I didn't know lies from the truth.

We had my old address and I went to work calling every bar within 15 miles. Cash figured my mom wouldn't work much farther away than that from her home, especially if she didn't have a car. I didn't realize she didn't have a car until Cash asked me about it. It was one of those things you don't think about but if my dad had killed her and we buried her, there would be *his* and *her* cars. It made me remember that we only had one.

Gosh, he was good!

I printed a list off and starting crossing off the bars that said "no" to my questions. It sort of went like this:

"Hey, I'm hoping you can help me. I'm looking for a woman who would have worked there about 13 years ago. Have you been open that long?"

If no, it was crossed out. If yes:

"Can I speak to someone who may have worked there at that time?"

Most of the time I had to leave a message. One time, I got the original owner and sometimes I got nowhere since most of the bars changed hands since then.

I told Cash that I was feeling despondent after I called seven bars with no luck.
He suggested something that changed everything.
"Stacey, people love a mystery. They really love being a part of something that everyone is going to talk about. They want to help with an "unsolved case" if they can. Crazy thing is they hate talking to cops. But they will probably do anything to talk to a daughter who is looking for her missing mom. Give them something and maybe they will give you something. Try calling those 7 bars again with that mindset."
I did. This time I said:
"Hey. This may sound crazy but my mom has been missing for 13 years. I knew she worked in a few different bars in the city of Beaufort. She was a drug addict but she was my mom and I'm just hoping for some answers."
I was surprised at how easily those words came out and how much I meant them. She *was* my mom. Even if I was pretty sure I knew she was dead, it would be nice to talk to someone who knew her and maybe had something good to say.
I was also surprised that Cash was right. Everyone wanted to help. The help poured out like a flood gate.
I got names and numbers of old bartenders and waitresses. I stayed on hold while new bar owners called their predecessors and daughters called their moms. Some jobs don't skip a generation.
I hit the jackpot and found 3 people I could talk to, but Cash was right. They wanted to meet me in person (probably to make sure I wasn't a cop).

CHAPTER 7: MOM'S "FRIENDS"

When Ruby found out that she knew the two other women who also knew my mom, she insisted that we all meet at *The Ranch*, a popular bar back in 2006-2007 where my mom hung out and "helped" on occasion. Ruby looked like someone who had a rough life, worked hard and made a few bad decisions. She had that raspy voice from smoking and had a gravelly laugh but when she spoke, it was nothing but sugar. I took to her immediately.

I got to the bar first and when Ruby walked in, she made a beeline for me and hugged me really tight. When she pulled back, she put her hands on my shoulders and looked me right in my eyes. She spoke with a country accent and seemed to really care about what she was about to say.

"Your mom was a scrapper. She did whatever she could to live every day. She was a self made lady who just got caught up in some bad stuff. It happens to the best people. I wish I knew who she could have been without the mess. I think she would have been really something to watch."

That was such an interesting way to describe someone, I thought.

It made me think about something Cash read to me about a house he was looking at. "Yeah, right," He said, reading the description out loud in a sweet rich woman voice "Here we

have a cozy, fixer upper located minutes from the heart of the city."
Then Cash said in his normal tone when he saw the address "That means it's a small, run down shack in the hood. Bring a weapon to the open house."
I thought Ruby did her best to "sell" my mom to me. From the horror stories my dad told, my mom was definitely a fixer-upper.
The other two ladies had come together and met us at the table.
"Sweetie, I knew your mom better than any of us and you look just like her, don't she, y'all?"
The other two laughed and nodded and one said "yeah, she was really pretty." But she kind of did her eye brows like there was a deeper meaning to that statement.
Since Cash thought it was best that he stayed outside and called the local police to set up a time to come in, I did this interview alone.
I wanted the ladies to know why I asked them there.
"Thank you guys so much for coming. My mother was no angel and I'm not here for fairy tales. I already know some of my mom's past, so you don't have to pretend she was someone she wasn't. If it helps, my father is Robert McClain and he was and still is just an awful man."
I decided not to be too revealing with what I thought I saw my dad do.
"I've got so many bad memories that I'm not sure what's what. My dad said she left with some guy but that's all I know. The last time I saw her was around 2007 or 2008 and I think she was asleep on the couch or in my bed. I remember them fighting but ..." I shook my head, dropped my jaw and laughed the laugh of something so painful that it was either laugh or cry. "Heh, I guess I remember her

sleeping a lot and I remember them fighting a lot. So I'm here. Anything you can tell me will help."

And that was all they needed. I sat in a hard chair at the round table in a bar where my mother sat 13 years ago. But, these ladies told me, my mother did not just sit. She raised Cain. That's southern talk for "excessive disruptive behavior."

If you had a boyfriend, he probably liked my mom. She drank, cussed, took money from the cash register before they fired her. She was caught doing drugs in the bathroom and got into bar fights.

My dad was the calmer of the two, if you can believe it. He would be called to come get her, pay for what she broke and her bar tab.

Everyone thought he did it because she was the mother of his child.

He would come into the bar in clothes that looked like he had been working. Ruby thought he worked nights at the saw mill but my dad was a private man who didn't share much so she felt bad for not knowing much about him. I understood her frustration. He was the only one they called because he was all she had. And no one wanted to deal with her.

She went from bar to bar, working or doing whatever to make money but *The Ranch* was her favorite hangout.

As with anyone you don't want around, when they don't come in for a while, you either forget them or just assume.

"I got another job and left, Tammy got married and I think Ruby - didn't you stay the longest? Sometimes I'd think about your mom but I kind of thought she got arrested or moved."

"I heard she left town. I didn't know she was missing. Gosh, it's been so long since I'd seen her, I don't remember when it was or what year."

We talked for a few more minutes about her lifestyle until I stood up. It was overwhelming. My mom was bound and determined to not have anything easy. Not her life or finding out what happened to her. No one knew if she had family alive besides me. Ruby said my mom said something about a sister but wasn't sure. In the end, I felt that it was a good chance no one had seen her after that night and if she was hiding out with a friend, these ladies would have seen her again in this bar. Although it was hard to hear, I felt confident that my mom did not stay in the area. Maybe she did leave with some guy and that memory I had of the train tracks was just a crazy dream.

I needed to know what my next steps were. I hugged and thanked the ladies and gave Ruby my cell. Cash would help me figure out where to go from here.

CHAPTER 8: LITTLE VICTORIES

Cash and I went inside the police station in South Carolina to talk to the detective he called earlier. Cash, like always, was prepared. "I've been talking to Detective Hill for a few weeks. He graciously put aside some time today for us."

"Yes, it's such an interesting case," Detective Hill said. "I actually was able to find out a few things with all the information Cash gave me a few weeks ago and just now when you called me with the old address, I found out even more. You say you want to be a detective, son?"

"Yes, sir. That's my dream."

"Well, you are on the right track, let me show you what I found."

We sat down to a folder with several old mug shots and about four pages of records.

"You gave me her parent's names so these records are for Robert McClain and Sherry Edwards. We have such a small county here that I knew this had to be her parents. Both have police records for domestic violence, drunk and disorderly and, um...your mother's record shows a history of..um."

"Prostitution", I said cutting him off. "My dad told me. He always called her a whore and said I probably wasn't his but he wasn't going to let her pimp raise me."

My face was red; I was sweating all of a sudden. I didn't know why. I was embarrassed. Why should I be, though? This wasn't me, Rae always said that. "They are not you!" What he said shocked me to my core.

"Um, no. Not at all. I was going to say drug possession. Nothing in here for soliciting or prostitution. Most of the time, drug use leads to it but even with your mom having a long record, I would think there would be one arrest for solicitation but there's not. She wasn't an angel but according to this file, she wasn't a prostitute."

Interesting.

Detective Hill continued. "Cash gave me your birthday and since you said that this happened when you were 7 or 8 years old, that would make the year of her disappearance either 2007 or 2008. I looked through her police records and her last arrest was in March of 2007. Now that doesn't mean much so I ran her social security number. This is where the pieces start coming together. There is no record of her after that arrest. I mean, if she moved away, her social was never run, so that means she never got a credit card or filled out a W4 for a job. Plus after years of being arrested, she suddenly got her life straight? It can happen but it does seem that she fell off the face of the Earth after March 2007. I also looked at missing persons and no one reported her missing. I also looked at unidentified remains and there was one woman who matched her description but she wasn't found by train tracks and it looks like that woman never had a child."

"Okay" I said listening.

Detective Hill closed the folder he was holding and put it on the desk. "I think you can fill out a missing persons report and we can start an investigation."

I smiled. Huge. No teeth. Cash quietly said "yes!"
I wasn't dreaming the night he woke me up. My father was a liar; she hadn't just left with "some guy". She was missing and I couldn't prove it but I knew she was dead.
It's hard to explain why we were happy.
I thought back to our early conversations we had when Cash was getting some "preliminary details" from me.
"Stacey, he said "Although this is something terrible and you're going to find out some horrible things, we've got to take time to celebrate little victories. I've read that investigations can be overwhelming, frustrating and exhausting. We will feel we aren't making any progress sometimes so let's remember to congratulate ourselves when something does go right"
We stood about five feet apart so that's what made what we did next so funny. Without even thinking, Cash and I "air" fived.

We filled out a missing persons report. But our short lived victory was coming to an end in 3, 2,
"One thing that's going to be hard is the evidence. Cash said you aren't sure where her body was buried but you do know it wasn't a far drive from your old home and it was by some railroad tracks a short walk from the road."
"*I* said all that?" I said trying to remember the details.
"Well, not exactly." Cash said "You told us what you knew and Detective Hill and I concluded that your dad didn't drive too far because you said it was dark when you left and returned. Most people hide bodies where they are familiar in a secluded area which means it was probably down tracks he must have used before. "
"And", Detective Hill chimed in "You said he put her body under a pile of something, I'm thinking that wasn't luck, he probably put the trash or whatever there. It could have been

unrelated to this crime, too. See, folks around here don't have too much money and when they are throwing out large items, they are supposed to take it to the dump where they have to pay to have it disposed. Your dad probably knew that area well and had made it his free dumping ground."

Now it was Cash's turn. "He also had to park close to the tracks since he was carrying dead weight and there's no easy place to park except for on the road. So we think we can find these tracks within a 10 miles radius."

"Wait." I said "Almost falling back a little. This is good news, right? "

Preparing my heart for a leap.

"Having you as a witness, I am hoping we can search for her", Detective Hill said.

But I knew there was something missing. I told you, I am always prepared for disappointment.

"We need some man hours and I'll try and get it approved".

Okay. I'm not getting it.

Cash took a deep breath. They looked at each other like they shared a secret.

"We think", Cash changed his gaze and looked right at me "We need your dad to take us to her".

CHAPTER 9: "CONNECT MY DEAD MOTHER TO MY LIVING FATHER"

As if on cue, my phone buzzed. It had been on silent the whole day. I needed sunshine and it was Rae.
"It's okay, tell Rae I said hi", Cash said. I made sure that whenever Rae called to check to see how the investigation was going, she was on speaker so we could update her. He always told her how strong I was. He told Rae that she was one of the reasons I had the courage to take this on but he made sure that she knew, the other reason was me. He told us one time that we often give credit to other people for our values when really it comes our inner strength. Rae added, "God gives us that inner strength and courage. Stacey was able to act on it with His help. And yours, Cash. We are blessed to have you."
I went to walk outside and realized I wasn't alone.
I mean, I had Rae but now I had another partner, someone who could speak for me. Cash looked at me and I gave him the phone without saying a word. I was in tears. "Hey Rae," Cash said "we need Stacey to do something incredibly brave

but possibly dangerous."
Rae laughed and said "Danger is her maiden name"
I laughed. My *maiden name*. It was an old private joke between us when I mixed up the two words "maiden and middle". Rae had challenged me to jump from this retention wall by our school when we were 12. It had to be 20 feet high and although I would hit the grass below, it would be a hard landing. Rae didn't do it; she said "it's too dangerous". I got to the top and confidently yelled
"danger is my maiden name!"
Rae always knew what to say.
Cash explained to both of us about the idea of me wearing a wire, maybe being kind to my father, and get him to talk. We needed a confession and we needed to find her body. He went on to explain that he and Detective Hill had talked about this at length. This little police department didn't have a "cold case" team, in fact, most cold case investigations were done by retired police officers. It would take a while to locate all the railroad tracks within ten miles of my home, but even then we would be guessing.
"Just say everything worked out and we found her body. Your dad could just tell the same tale he's been telling - your mom left with some guy and that guy probably killed her." As odd as it is, since it's been so long, a slam dunk would be for him to show us (me) where exactly she was buried. That way the defense wouldn't have much of a case, especially if he admitted it."
Maybe I would finally get answers.
But how? I didn't talk to my father; I would occasionally go to his house to make sure he wasn't dead. The years had not been kind to him, but he had not been kind to his years. Heavy drinking, smoking, whatever drugs he did or was still doing, not eating right or taking care of himself made

him a bitter, old man who was only 49 years old. He had an injury at work and they gave him some money. I think he did odd jobs but I didn't know. He didn't spend a lot, I guess, so I would go by once a month and buy him some stuff to make sandwiches.

I think I told myself that I was a Christian so I should act like it. It did not come from a place of love or even guilt. God blessed me so I occasionally passed it on. It was so much easier giving to the orphans than this sorry excuse for a father. I did it begrudgingly but I "told "God that this was the best I could do so take it or leave it. I was soon to discover that God had bigger plans than my once a month run to the grocery store for this other child of his.

When Cash finished talking, Rae was quiet. I had so many questions and I was petrified of wearing a wire. I just kind of rambled about how my dad hated police and liars and here I was about to combine the two in his living room.

I didn't know how to start or what to say. How do I even begin? "Hey dad, I know you killed mom, can you tell me how and where you buried her? Oh speak up into my shirt please, thanks."

Oh, and the ramifications of my actions if I tricked and deceived him. Do not think I understand how you're feeling. Yes, this horrible man probably killed my mother and made me help bury her, so who cares about what he might say to me? He would be in jail. But my mind went back to that scared little Stacey who never wanted to have any confrontation with anyone, let alone this man. His words and evil stare would hit me like a fist. Just the idea of seeing him in court made my heart race and that is only if things went right!

What if things went wrong? Would he kill me for dragging his name in open court and accusing him of murder? I can't do it.

I said all of this and finally stopped talking.

Cash had the phone still on speaker. Rae spoke "Stacey, let me pray for you".

I bowed my head, still thinking about all the problems that could happen and it didn't even occur to me that praying could make Cash uncomfortable. I mentioned church one time but it didn't seem to come up on his end and I didn't want to ask him too many personal questions. But Rae didn't hide her flame of faith under a bush ("oh no! I'm gonna let it shine!") I wasn't as strong as her, praying for something like this came easy to her, I thought. My first response to a life changing question was fear, doubt and worry, Rae's was prayer.

I looked at Cash and his head was bowed, eyes closed so I quickly did the same, I didn't want him to catch me looking. Rae took a breath and prayed "God, You said when two or three are gathered in your name you are with us. Thank You for being with us now."

That actually made me feel better. I believed what God said but only when it helped me or if I thought it could but Rae reminded me that God was there. He wasn't in some far away land, He was with us.

She continued. "Lord, we come to you because your child Stacey has to make a decision and she doesn't know what to do. Lord, this is so big that you need to slap her with the answer."

Rae. She talked to God like He was her friend. Just like she would talk to me. It made it easier to listen to her pray than some of the preachers I've heard.

"God, please make it easy. Remove any doubt from her mind if this is something You want her to do. She's had it so hard, but it's because of that life that she is so strong.

Please, make it obvious and easy. If it's not in Your will to make it easy, then surround her with strength and peace. In Jesus name, amen"
"Amen".
"Slap her with the answer?" Cash asked laughing. "Okay"
Rae just said "yup. With something this big, she needs to know without a doubt that it's the right thing and it's coming from God. Everything in life doesn't need to be hard. This is hard enough."
"So you want God to slap her? Huh?" Cash joked.
Rae just laughed. "Ask and ye shall receive"

We thanked Detective Hill and said we would be in touch.
We drove back to Savannah without talking about the plan. Rae's prayer was still on my mind. It was so comforting to know I didn't need to make a decision right away. In fact, I slept so peacefully because as weird as it sounds, the decision wasn't up to me anymore. I literally gave the decision to God.
I had waited 13 years. *Waited* isn't even a good word for it, I carried this burden, I held this secret, I shamed myself and placed this boulder on my back for 13 years. It affected everything in my life! I didn't pray about it, and I didn't have peace. Now faced with this monumental choice, you would think I would be up all night, pondering, worrying, and asking myself "what do I do?"
Making my famous list of "pros and cons".
But no, not tonight. As I lay down, I grabbed my favorite squishy pillow and I pulled a "Rae".
I talked to God like a friend. "It's your crap now, you deal with it."
But I said it reverently. I was still for a minute and I said it again but this time *knowing*.
Just knowing that God would take care of it.

Tears filled my eyes.
 "God, thank you for dealing with this. Thank you"
I smiled and fell asleep.
I felt so at peace I didn't even wake up to the pounding at my door.

CHAPTER 10: ASK AND YOU SHALL RECEIVE

My alarm went off at 9am. I loved sleeping in and that day I felt so refreshed that the pounding on the door seemed to blend into the background. It grew louder and more persistent until I realized that someone was about to break it down.
Everyone else in the house was already at work, Rae and her parents. I was the only one who had the morning off before I went into class. The pounding didn't stop and I got scared. I ran to the window but didn't see a car and from my angle I couldn't see a person either. I thought I'd try and hide until I heard an awful, yes awfully familiar voice. "I need to talk to Stacey. Now."
It was my father.

This couldn't be happening so fast, just yesterday we talked to the detective about wearing a wire. I didn't have time to think about a plan or even call Cash. This wasn't supposed to happen like this. I was shaking and scared but my father was not a man you made wait for any length of time and my time was running out. I grabbed my phone, yelled to the door "hang on a sec", and texted Cash three words.

"Dad is here".

I threw on a sweatshirt over my pajama top and opened the door, like I just woke up and had no earthly idea why he was there.

He stepped back. Neither of us said "hi".

"Get out here" he said and stepped back so I had room.

"What do you want; I'm getting ready to go to school." I stayed in the doorway.

"Get out here, you don't want the people you're living with knowing your business."

The "people" I've been living with for the last three years, since I was 17, had names and he knew them all but never once called them anything but "Bible thumpers or church-lovers or them-fancy-insert-cuss-word-here-snobs".

But it dawned on me that he didn't know I was alone and that made me feel safe. I acted like they were at the top of the stairs behind me and called up to them "Yeah, I'm okay. Its just my dad. Sorry he woke you."

Ugh, was that too much? I was laying it on pretty thick.

He motioned for me to follow him to his ratty car and said "they ain't at work?"

"Um, her dad works from home"

He didn't of course.

This made my dad's day. "Pansy. Too good to get his hands dirty"

He got in the driver's side. I opened the passenger door but didn't get in.

"I've got to go to school"

"We aint going for a drive. Get in"

I sat in that nasty car. It was dirty and smelled like an ashtray. Cheerwine bottles half filled with cigarette butts and old soda. Trash and grease stains on the carpet and seats. He didn't even clear off the crap I was about to sit on

and I dared not touch it.
I didn't say a word.
"I heard you went to *The Ranch* and been asking about your sorry mama?"
This was it. Showtime! There would be no rehearsal, we are going live. Without a wire or any recording device. Really, God? This is happening.
But when I opened my mouth to speak, the words came out easily and strangely enough, truthfully. I mean, I left out the train tracks and some minor details that only I needed to know but I sat there and said without so much as a quiver in my voice that there had been a missing person's report filed on my mom. I told him that I went to South Carolina to see if the people she used to work with had seen her and that I told them that I had always heard she left with some guy.

This calmed him. I guess somewhere in the back of his mind he thought I might have remembered the train tracks and the burial. When I said the story he had told me all those years, he might of felt like he was in the clear. Yeah. But my dad is a careful and crafty man.
He looked at me and asked if they had called me.
Now I don't care about lying to a liar and I think God would forgive me if I did but I didn't really have to. Cash had called me, right? I mean I called him too but in this case, it worked.
"Yes, dad. A police officer investigating the case called me".
This was almost easy.
"And?"
"Dad, there's so much I need to tell you but I seriously have to go to class."
And then I added for good measure:
"Where can we talk where no one can listen in?"

I was almost excited. I had him with that!
I used my dad's own paranoia to help me.
If he thought *I* didn't want to be recorded, he would feel safe talking, right?
But I couldn't let him think about anything too long or he would get suspicious and call it off.
But he came to me so he wants to know what I know.
"Meet me at my house then." He said.
"Okay. I'll be in class at ten for about an hour or so um so I'll be there in about two and a half hours. Want me to pick up lunch from Betty's?"
I knew he loved their fried chicken and I needed to buy myself some time and give him something to look forward to.
"Fine" he said gruffly. "Make fancy man pay for it"
My dad loved to get over on someone.
"Okay. See you at 12 or so"
He left.
I ran inside to get my phone which had 14 missed calls and 5 urgent text messages, all from Cash.

He answered on the first ring. He told me he was already headed to my house since all he got was my last ominous text.
"No, don't come here…I mean, sorry." I was trying to catch my breath. I took short breaks between words as I ran inside. "He came here because (breath) someone told him we were talking about my mom and (breath) I don't think he thinks I remember anything. Anyway, (big deep breath) I'll tell you about it but can you get the wiring device and get that set up on me? He wants to talk. I have to get chicken."
"You're getting chicken?" he said confused "Okay, Stace. I'll take care of all of it.

I'll meet you wherever."

On the way to meet Cash at the police station, I realized just how fast God worked and how strangely different I felt from yesterday. Yesterday was an unknown. I would have never imagined that the answer to my prayers last night would be my dad pounding on my door but I learned more in his few words this morning in 13 minutes than I learned from him in the last 13 years. But that conversation wouldn't have happened without our investigation.

Today I wasn't scared of my dad hurting me and I wasn't scared of confronting him.

I was ready for this to be over. We had done as much as we could, this could not have happened without Cash. Thank God someone left their keys on his desk, he may not have ran after me in that parking lot.

I thought back to just 2 months ago when this began.

I didn't have the confidence when we first started this like I have now.

During our trips to South Carolina and back, Cash would tell me how much easier it is for officers to interrogate suspects when they knew the answers to the questions. So a few months ago, I didn't know if she was actually missing nor did I know that her paperwork trail ended in March of 2007.

Having this information, I felt like I was armed and ready for the attack.

Whatever my dad was going to throw at me, I had this armor of information to shield myself from his lies and I can fire back with the truth.

Not only was I ready, I was excited.

CHAPTER 11: CHICKEN AND HALF TRUTHS

I met Cash and he hooked me up with a small microphone. It wasn't like in the movies, he said I could even put it on the lid of a soda bottle. He reached into his car and handed me two Cheerwines and two packs of salted nuts.

"I thought this might help."

Without thinking, I threw my arms around him and all of a sudden, all my emotions just poured out. I do not cry.

And so I cried for all the times I never cried.

I wept for my mom, her decisions and her sad life.

I cried for my dad, knowing that he must have been hurt too because no one could have been that mean and angry without abuse.

I cried hard for me. I felt sorry for myself, crappy parents, no friends. I didn't deserve that.

But after the heavy, gut wrenching cries -you know the kind- where no one talks to you because your sobs would drown out any words - came the deep breaths of appreciation.

My thoughts then turned to thankfulness. I cried because Cash was such a good guy. He took his own personal time to help me and he listened. He bought me Cheerwines to help establish trust with my dad. Who does that?

I cried because my Rae of sunshine had been the best friend anyone could have asked for. I found myself thankful for so much more than I had felt pity for.

I thanked God for my salvation and bringing my friend Rae into my life that reminded me to simply "give that crap to God". He can work miracles.

I pulled back, wiped my eyes and looked down and took a breath.

Cash simply said "you've got this."

There was a mic on me and one on the Cheerwine.

My dad still lived in South Carolina so it was going to take me about 30 minutes to get to his house and I still needed to grab Betty's chicken.

Cash and his partner followed me with the blessing and cooperation with the detective from his precinct.

Like I said, Cash was always prepared. He had been filling in his partner and officers at work with what he was doing in his spare time.

They gave him advice and were eager to follow alongside our journey. He had briefed them a little this morning from our weekend adventure so when I texted Cash at 9am "dad is here", he already had an army of officers prepared for the wire tapping and ride along.

I felt safe knowing Cash and his partner would follow me to my dad's house but would stay out of sight. These mics work like cell phones so I didn't know how the service or transmission was going to be in my dad's trailer but we thought the best idea would be to talk a little first and go to the bathroom and text Cash to see if he could hear okay.

Betty's chicken made this easy. Dad and I had a small conversation about how good it was and how you couldn't find anything like it anywhere.

I told dad I had a surprise for him and handed him the Cheerwine with peanuts.

He pushed them aside and said "it's only good on road trips."

So I put mine (mic'd up one) on the table and put his in the fridge.

I fixed him a plate of just chicken and just went into the bathroom to wash my hands.

I texted Cash.

He wrote back "only good on road trips" and I knew he could hear everything.

He also wrote back "text or call anytime, I'm one min away. You got this."

I looked in the mirror, prayed to God for words and strength. I prayed that this would be easy.

I walked out and sat at the small, wobbly cluttered kitchen table.

We started to eat in silence but I stopped.

"Dad. I'm going to pray for our meal"

He didn't bow his head, I knew he wouldn't but he did stop chewing which was a start.

"Thank you God for this meal. Thanks for my dad. Please help us through this."

When I looked up, my dad's eyes were red. I was used to this because he drank and they were usually blood shot but this time it was different.

I was going to let him speak first but I decided I couldn't wait.

"Dad, I need you to take me to my mom. I want to put flowers on her grave. I hate that she's been out there all this time. She didn't deserve that."

With that sentence, I let him know I knew everything.

Maybe that was a mistake because the red eyes that may have been from tears, were now from anger.
"You know what she deserved? A good kick in her...that whore. Piece of garbage. She got the police called on me, I almost lost my job, and you almost got put in a home. You didn't know her. "
I stood up. I started to yell.
"And I never will, because of you! What did I deserve, dad? A life without a mother or a good father? A life of horrible memories? You didn't let me have any friends or go anywhere. You are a mean, angry jerk. I deserved a better life.
You killed my mother and you made me help you bury her! Why did you wake me up? Do you know what that did to me my whole life? Then you lied to me! I thought I dreamed it, I thought I was crazy."
I was so loud. I had been silent long enough. I wanted to shout it from the rooftops. He had never seen me like that before.
"You don't know anything." he said coldy.
"You know what? I don't know a lot but I actually know why you killed her. Pick any reason, dad, she was a whore, a druggie, liar, worthless, whatever. So I get it. I actually understand why you killed her but", my voice got lower, and "what I don't understand ...
 (I was almost whispering in an angry sinister voice) "Is why you woke me up?"
I glared at him. To the fly on the wall, I was angrier about that than the murder of my mom.
 He looked at me. He was angry too.
I stared at him.
 Then I really looked at him.
Then I tried to see him like God would. His son. His sad,

broken son.

I softened my voice. "Please, why did you wake me up and make me carry that shovel?"

His words weren't angry anymore. He pushed the plate away. He breathed deep and confessed.

"The day before I got a call at my job at midnight from the neighbor. You knocked on their door to see where your parents were. The neighbor, Mandy or Brandy that old busy body said (his voice mimicking the neighbor) *"Your daughter is at my house looking for her mommy and daddy. She's hungry and I'm going to call the police you sorry excuse for a man.* Your mom was supposed to be there, she was passed out on the couch when I left. The neighbor said when she tried to take you back to our house to check it out, that it was dirty and it was disgusting. She told me that if she ever found you wandering around in the streets in the middle of the night, she would call child services."

I had never heard him talk so much in my life but maybe we were alike. Once it started to come out, it didn't stop. I was glued to the edge of my seat.

"I left work early, my boss was ticked and I couldn't tell him that my sorry ex wife left our daughter alone. This wasn't the first time you were left alone either but I couldn't have cops involved."

I knew he never married my mom. I think the name "exwife" was just easier to describe his situation with her.

"So I met Mandy or Brandy at my house and had to hear her chew me up and spit me out. I had to just take it from that sorry busy body. She knew all my business and she told me her whole family was watching me.

I was angry but I didn't know where your mom was so I couldn't go back to work. I took you to school the next day and I got ready for my night shift. I called everyone

and they told me she left with some guy. Your mom finally showed up, drunk and she passed out on the couch.
I didn't even talk to her because she was out so I finished getting ready. I made you a sandwich for after school and I left."

There were a few things I thought he lied about but slowly they started to ring a sense of familiarity. *Candy* was the neighbor's name. I can't believe I remembered it but when you're 7 and your neighbor's name is Candy, it's pretty cool. In fact, I changed the name of one of my Barbie dolls to Candy.
The sandwich, I thought that was a lie but something on his counter triggered a memory. Peanut butter and honey. My dad knew a guy that gave us fresh honey so dad saved money on jelly. He would make me a sandwich and by the time I would eat it, the bread would be kind of hard from the air hitting it.
When you're a kid, and sandwiches magically appear, you don't think that someone who cared about you made it. You just see it, grab it, sit by the TV and eat it, but that's the best thing about being a kid. No worries.

My dad continued.
"I went to work. I got another call that night around 8 or so but it was you calling. My boss had to call me off a job to come all the way to the phone since my cell didn't have service out in the field. It took me about 15 minutes to get to the office and you were crying. Your mom left again and it was storming. You said all the electricity went out so you got scared and called me."
How could I forget that? He was right. I remember I looked all over for a flashlight to look at my dad's cell and work numbers on the fridge. I finally found a light up toy I had

and I used it to see.
I remember calling and asking to speak with Mr. Robert.

"It took another 30 minutes for me to get home. When I left my job, my boss said that this was the last time or I wouldn't be coming back. Your mom wasn't just costing me time and money, but if this kept happening, you were going to be put in foster care. I remember that the traffic light was out by our house so I figured a tree limb landed on an electric line. When I got inside the house, the lights were still out and you were on the couch. I told you to go to bed. When you got to your room, you said your mom was in your bed. I went to wake her up but she was passed out so I carried her to the couch."

Nope. A lie. Well, maybe not a total lie, just lies like the devil tells, half truths. My eyes were darting now, trying to remember. I think that finally, with his memory and mine, we might get to what really happened.

My dad was such an angry man that there was no way to know when certain things happened on specific days. So now I knew, this happened the night she died.

I stopped him. "No, that's not what happened. Yes, you came home angry and told me to go to bed. But when I came back out to tell you she was in my bed, you started yelling and cussing at me. Then you stormed into my room in the dark and grabbed mom by her hair and drug her still in her sleeping bag into the living room. I got scared and ran into my room and cried myself to sleep. I forgot that you doing that happened that same night . A few hours later you woke me up to help bury her after you had killed her.

Oh man.", I sat down again. I looked him square in his face. "You really killed her."

CHAPTER 12: THE TRUTH

I didn't know why I was shocked that I finally got the answer I had known all along. All the pieces came together. Maybe I didn't even need to get him to take me to her dead body, he just confessed.
And then he didn't.
"I didn't kill her. When I took her to the living room.."
("Took", that sounded a lot better than "when I dragged her by her hair to the living room")
"She was limp. I thought she had passed out in your bed but I didn't know when she got there or how long she had been there. She should have got up. It was a bad lightning storm and the flashes would light the trailer. She was slumped in the bag and it was wet. I think she overdosed and threw up. I tried to shake her and rolled her on her stomach. I kept shaking her and slapping her face. I didn't know what to do."

I kept picturing my dad shaking her and the flashes of light showing her face and going dark again. I imagined my dad's anger turning into fear then full on panic.
He stopped. He said what anyone in his place 13 years ago would have said "I got scared. She was dead."
My dad sat there for a minute and said "I kept thinking that I was in trouble. If I called the police, I would definitely

be arrested for murder since I have a record for domestic violence. Even if I was found not guilty, you'd be taken away no matter what. Brandy or Mandy would tell her stories; she had plenty of them since she was our neighbor and heard the fights. For just a brief moment, all the lights came back on and I saw that she had that death look. I never saw it before but you know it when you do. She had been dead for a while. I've thought about that night a lot. Why didn't you know she was home? I think you didn't see her when you called me. She was probably in your bed the whole day. You just ate your sandwich and watched TV.
Also, she was cold. She had been dead for a while. I went to your room to see if you were asleep and I thought about what I should do. I turned the hallway light on and that's when I saw the needle. You could have stepped on it. She was getting high in your room, in your bed. What kind of mother does that? What if you had stepped on that needle? I was so angry. That's when I decided that although I could prove she had overdosed, I knew they would put you in foster care because of my record and how crappy the trailer was and there was no way to prove those weren't my drugs. I didn't want you to wake up again and go to the neighbors so I got you, got the shovel and we buried that piece of garbage.
She didn't even deserve that. And no, I'm not going to her grave again for you to put flowers there. Now you know."

I sat there, taking it all in, finally remembering parts I thought were gone.
"I did see her, dad. I got home and no one was there. I think I ate my sandwich and watched TV. I remember going into my room and seeing her. I remember thinking she was sick because she was in her sleeping bag and there was throw up in it. I don't really remember when I called you but the

lights had all gone out and I tried to wake her up. I had to find that spinning thing that lit up so I could see. It was in my toy box. Yeah, I got it out of the toy box and was spinning it around. I was scared but mostly I wanted the tv back on."
Man, I couldn't believe I remembered so much. Like I said before, my normal day was anger, yelling and a passed out mom. No wonder I needed dad's story to help finish mine.
I went on "So, I called your number and I remember somebody was really mad so I pretended to cry and I said mom wasn't here. That way you would come home and fix the lights so I could watch TV again."
Dad, I'm sorry I lied that night. I bet it made you even angrier and even worried you would lose your job."
His face softened a little.
"You were just a kid," he said.

"Just take me there." I begged. "It will give me some closure."

He looked at me. We shared a secret. I think he was exhausted not just from this conversation but from the years of hiding it. In that brief moment, he gave up and I jumped on it.
"I don't care anymore. Get my drink."
I got the Cheerwine and nuts out of the fridge.
"Not that one. That's for you."
I then grabbed what I knew he wanted a beer for the road. I got in the front seat to drive, not knowing what was going to happen next. I still had both mics on but by now I wasn't even sure if there was a crime besides hiding a body? Would Cash and his partner jump out and arrest him when we got to the tracks?
What would my dad be charged with? He never lied to the

police since there was never an investigation.
So many questions went through my head as he pointed left or right. We took a series of turns and I wish I had a second to look at my phone but I couldn't. If I had, I would have seen several texts from Cash while I was interrogating my dad.
"Good job"
"Keep him talking"
"I'm sorry"
And lastly:
 "We are behind you."

Cash had already installed a tracking device on my phone just for this day so they didn't have to follow too closely.
I think he knew by now, I wasn't scared; I just wanted this to be over. She didn't need to stay under that crap any longer. No sin deserves that kind of burial especially for this long.

My dad pulled over by a school and got out. He walked down the white rocky side of the train tracks still drinking his beer.
We walked in silence for about 10 minutes. I imagined that it felt longer for him with a 120 lb dead woman in a

sleeping bag on his back. We walked past a warning sign and he stopped. That's another answered question. No wonder he knew exactly where to find her. If your "sign" is an actual sign, it was easy to find. The warning sign probably was lit up at night.
"There", he pointed to a trash pile.
There it was. After 13 years of rain, heat, old trash and new growth were the remains (bad choice of words) of an

old, ratty mattress along with tires and so much random garbage that no one would ever think this was a burial ground instead of the dumping ground that it was.
It was both. It was heartbreaking. Somewhere under that garbage were the remains of a woman who's life was full of promise. I thought about God and how His heart must be breaking too. Unlike us, He knew her potential, He knew what she could have been and like us, He watched her throw it away, just like she was thrown away. The irony, sadness, stillness and disappointment was almost too much.
I just stood there. I didn't even bring any flowers.
I expected some sort of gruff comment of degradation to my mom but he surprised me.
"I'm sorry, Sherry" he was tough for a minute and then his voice broke. "I'm so sorry Sherry."
His shoulders started to shake and he held his head in his hands. He was broken. Years and years of carrying this weight had taken a toll on him. His anger was coming out in tears and he started to really cry. As angry as I was, I felt bad for him. I felt sorry that he had to carry this burden. The assumption of murder from his own daughter when in his own twisted mind, he did this for me.
I put my arm around him. We both stood there crying.
He said something else which shocked me again.
"We've got to get her out of here."

For a brief moment I really thought he was going ask me to dig her up and rebury her somewhere nicer. Don't forget, my dad hated police but God continued to answer prayers.
"I'll tell them everything I know", he said.

"Them" was police. I took him back to his house and I immediately went outside so my dad couldn't hear and called Cash who was on standby.

"Please, I begged. He's doing this on his own volition. Can you not arrest him in front of everyone in his neighborhood? Can we come in to the station?"

Of course, Cash being Cash, told me he had already arranged it with Detective Hill in South Carolina. We would meet as soon as I could get him back in the car.
I didn't want my father to sleep on anything and change his mind. We drove right there. I let him grab another beer for the road but made him have some gum for his breath.
To be honest, I let him do all the talking. He told it in his own words and of course left out anything that made him look bad. I thought to myself that it didn't have any bearing on what we came to do. We needed to unearth my mother, give her a decent burial, close a day old missing person's case and end a 13 year old mystery.

CHAPTER 13: HE WINS AND LOSES

Cash and I sat behind my father in court for his sentencing. Rae and her family were behind us. My father opted for a bench trial, which is where your fate is decided by a Judge and not a jury. This case didn't get much attention and he was the last on the docket so we were pretty much alone when it came his time to stand in judgment, except for one local reporter.

When the police found my mother's remains with the help of my father, the cause of death was "undetermined".

My father lied so much that I anxiously awaited the coroner's report to see if it actually was a homicide and maybe I had been hugging a murderer after all. The State could not believe that a man with a domestic violence record could have "just buried" the body of his ex girlfriend that he had *not* killed. They wanted to charge him with homicide but the medical examiner indicated that there were no knife marks or bullet wounds on the bones. She had simply degraded so much that there was very little evidence left. But obvious signs of murder were not there. Plus she had a history of drug use so his story was checking out.

The other thing that worked in his favor was just coming forward. The State agreed that she wasn't even missing so my dad testifying against himself was what the case was built on.

In the end, he was charged with "preventing the lawful burial of a body."

It came with 2 years in prison and 5 years probation but the judge did something unheard of. He had listened to my story and how Cash and I got it this far and he looked at me and said

"Without you, young lady, we wouldn't be here. What do you think we should do with your dad?"

I had thought about his punishment for a long time before the judge ever asked me that. Again, God gave me the strength to speak.

"Your honor, my father lives in a rundown trailer and his health is failing. He has no one besides me. If you put him in prison, he will get nutritious hot meals and be forced to clean his cell, maybe even make a friend. On the other hand, if he remains free, he will be in prison in his own home but on his own terms. Either way he wins and either way he loses."

I looked over at the man that had been a monster to me and I expected him to look angry or even broken but what I saw made me trust in God even more. My dad looked relieved. His body was standing taller like he was ready to accept any punishment that he deserved but the heavy weight he had been emotionally carrying was gone. You could see it in his face, demeanor and overall body language. He was polite to the judge and was very mannerly. He answered every question with "Yes, sir " or "No, sir". He was honest when he was asked about his past drug use and any abuse he had done to my mom. Things came out that weren't supposed to because he was just letting it all out. It got so bad that his court appointed

attorney would try and stop him from adding things he didn't have to share. In this case, it worked in his favor.
The judge was impressed by his candor and felt that he and my mom had abused one another and sadly, me too. The judge told me that if I wasn't doing something in this field or at least help others, I was wasting my God-given talent.
The judge eventually decided that he needed court mandated counseling with someone that I chose plus the mandatory probation but no prison time. Then the judge said we should do some sessions jointly. Counseling with my dad?
I never thought I'd see the day.
I chose a Christian counselor with Rae's help.
My relationship with my dad will never be like; I was about to say "normal" but what's normal anyway?
If you have a good relationship with your dad, please don't take it for granted.

Dad didn't have a lot but he paid for a small headstone for mom without being forced. Cash told a local news station about it (with my blessing) and donations were able to cover what my dad couldn't.

Over the next few months, changes took place in every aspect of my life.
First, I changed courses (and colleges) and decided to become a therapist and maybe even get a degree in psychology. I started with a plan to create my own Christian-based business on helping people talk throuhg their trauma. It was a new type of therapy that I came up with on my own. "Drive and Chat" . We just drive and chat. Maybe go to the places that hold good and bad memories for people who needed to get something off their chest. It worked wonders for me.

Something really strange happened between me and my dad. Since this all came out, I didn't look at him as a liar anymore and because I was on my own, he looked at me as an independent, confident young adult who he helped raise that way. I began to understand him more, especially through the psychology classes I was taking. My professor was a former psychiatrist and she would take time to have lunch with me and explain how I had to find his "love language" and that I needed to see *me* from his point of view. It truly helped that I was now going to a Christian college.

Here's a great example of the first time I was able to stop, think one way and actually change my thought process.

Whenever Cash could, he would attend church with me and Rae and her family. One day, I decided to invite my father to church and I told him that we would go out with Rae's family afterwards to a local restaurant. I told him that either Rae's family or Cash never had Betty's chicken and I needed help convincing them to go and drive an extra 15 minutes away.

After some persuading, he met me at my house and her dad drove us all to church. Dad was a man of few words except about things he was an expert at.

He talked about Betty's fresh, crispy mouth-watering food that you thought he was in a commercial. We went to church together and the pastor talked about the prodigal son. If you don't know, this wealthy father had 2 sons and one went off and spent his inheritance on wine, women and song until he was broke and eating what the pigs he was taking care of were eating. When he returned, his father was overjoyed because he would always look at the end of the road waiting for him to return.

When we got in the car after the sermon, my dad said "that

story was like yours, when you came home."
So, my first thought was "Really? You seriously think I'm that son who left a good, loving father to waste my money on frivolous and harmful vices only to come back to the open arms of a dad who missed and loved me? You need hearing aids because you missed everything."
But I just looked out the window, pretty angry until he spoke again.
"Yeah, I thought you were gone for good but you came back and gave me a chance to tell my side."
Hmmm, okay. Not exactly what I got from it but hey, it was something. I needed to not jump to conclusions. *My dad went to church and he listened and took away something good. Baby steps for both of us.*
Then I really got a chance to change my thinking when we got our food.
The server asked us if we needed anything and he said, pointing at me, "ask her, that's my daughter. She's in college and she knows what this chicken needs."
Perfect example right here.
My first thought was to shake my head and apologize for whatever that was but instead I tried to look at that sentence from my father's perspective.
Before I analyzed it, though, the server was waiting for an answer which I had been told a hundred times, "yes," I said with a smile "this chicken needs your famous hot sauce and honey."
"Y'all must be locals." She said "I'll grab some for everyone."
While my dad told Cash and Rae and her family between bites and while pieces of chicken skin escaped from his mouth every now and then about how you weren't supposed to pour it on, just dip it "oh, no, the honey goes into the bowl first then the hot sauce then the honey.

Always more honey than hot sauce."

I watched him and I thought about the statement he made about me to our server.

"That's my daughter (he is acknowledging that he is my father, he's not embarrassed of me)

"She's in college" (he's proud of my accomplishments)

"Ask her what this chicken needs". (I was also an expert, his equal. We finally were on the same level.)

When we went back to the conversation, I felt good about myself. Hate is slippery and sometimes it can be easy to hold when the other person is hot-headed and hot tempered but it can also hard to hold on to when you think that the person you're supposed to hate is bringing some sweet stuff. In his own way, my dad was bringing the honey and he was making it hard to hold that hate.

Some of the things he was going to say could be taken either way and really it was up to me to decide. So I chose the honey. You can keep the hot sauce. I was done being burned.

CHAPTER 14: NEWS

Cash and I became really good friends. People would ask if we were "dating" but we just rode around, ate, and talked just like we did during the investigation so I didn't know how to answer it.

As always, Cash was prepared.
"I've been thinking about you a lot, your parents, your life, and your faith."

Before I finish that story, let me jump in real quick. My faith became a lot stronger since the answered prayers and in my mind, the miracle with my dad. I totally changed my perspective, I prayed a lot more, went to church and gave a lot of things to God.

I didn't rush relationships and I was anxious to see what God held in store for me, not just what I wanted in life. I really wanted to help people. Cash started to take notice and would pray before our meals with me. Cash would watch how prayer and church sermons would make us think. My dad always said something about the sermon; sometimes he didn't understand it and Rae's dad always had a way of explaining things so no one felt stupid.

One day Dad said he was tired of being behind and he wanted to know what the preacher was going to talk about the next week. He called me and he was on a roll. "I just wish I had a book or something that could tell me what I'm supposed to know before we just show up."

I started to laugh. "You want a book? About God and what a preacher might reference? I guess it would have to be a really *good book*."
I laughed at my own joke again.
"Dad, I think you want a bible."
"I don't want to read that whole long thing, he scoffed, "I just want that cliff notes one and I want to know what the preacher is going to talk about. Like your college. I'm tired of not understanding."
My father loved to read. He was not stupid, he had worked heavy machinery and he always read about safety and taught other guys after him. He read a lot about history, his favorite time was ancient Greece and Rome. He knew a lot about Christian persecution by the Romans. He always remarked about how Rome was so powerful and yet, it fell. No one living in Rome at that time would believe what happened. I felt the same way about kid Stacey. But the opposite of Rome. I wish I could have told her that in the future, "things will be so much better, little girl that you're even going to want to visit dad! Just wait little Stacey, things aren't going to be bad forever."
I connected my dad with the pastor. I didn't know how it worked, when does a pastor know what he's going to talk about? Do they shoot from the hip? Do they prepare months out for a series? My dad got to know him and another miracle happened, the pastor would prepare his sermon *with* my father! My father would ask questions and the pastor would take into account that not everyone understood exactly what he was saying. The pastor would then answer the questions in his sermon. Now, that was beyond my realm of comprehension. It was better than what I could imagine.

Dad and I talked a few times a week about the classes I

was taking and he loved to hear about psychology and even my boring assignments. I even started to go to his trailer to study because he liked helping me find the answers in my textbooks. I also brought my laptop and he helped me with online searches and essays I had to write.

Cash was studying too. He wanted to be a detective more than anything but he had to take exams and classes. Helping solve my mom's case had connected him to some higher ups so he was put on a fast track of being one of the youngest detectives on the force but it would not happen overnight.

Cash would come to my dad's trailer with me and study. My dad's hatred of police was nonexistent now and Cash and him became fast friends, bonding over the GA Bull Dogs and police business. To hear my dad ask questions about cases and procedures always made me look over at them, shake my head, then back to my project.

Another strange thing started to happen. Since dad was having weekly visitors and sometimes we would get in his car to run errands, he began to clean up. The house didn't have that weird smell of cigarettes and old beer. The table was always cleared off and the counters weren't sticky. He still smoked but didn't do it inside anymore and he decided to not smoke at all in his car. I bought him new floor mats and he took it to a car wash and we both got the car inside pretty nice.

He also slowed down on his drinking. He was a work in progress and every week he would tell us that he had one less cigarette or beer than the week before. Dad had a goal chart on his fridge. It was cute and funny because the only one they had in the store was for little kids doing chores so it had little lines and smiley faces and little bears all over it. I laughed when I saw it but smiled really proudly when I

saw these black hash marks next to a yellow teddy bear that said:
Week 1 "Cigs": he had made a tally mark for every cigarette he had that week starting on Sunday.
Week one I counted 142. That's about a pack a day.
Week two I counted 140.
Week three he smoked 137.
He also wrote next to the green bear "beer".
It was also progress.
Week one he drew 23 hash tags. About 3 beers a day.
Week two, he had 20
Week three was only 14.

Oh, I forgot, speaking of projects, the pastor called me one day to ask me something. My dad and him had become really good friends over that last 6 months. I knew they were talking and having lunches every now and then but I didn't know just how close they were.
"Your dad said it was okay to talk to you, Stacey. He has had a lot of questions for me and I've done the best I could to answer them, sometimes I had to bring in reinforcements."
"Yeah, my dad doesn't do anything without knowing what it all entails. He doesn't do "faith" very well."
"Right", said the pastor "but I love skeptics! They make the best Christians because they have more than faith, they have found enough proof so they know it's real. I mean, people don't realize it but there is so much evidence out there proving Jesus died and he was the son of God. Your dad asked me about miracles, the Old Testament and New. He wanted to know why it may seem like a loving God doesn't seem to answer prayers or help everyone in need."
"Yeah, I've wondered that myself," I said.
"Well, God gives us free will and He doesn't control us.

He wants us to do the right things and He even gave us instructions or commandments like "love one another" and "judge not" and "give your tithes to the church". People think the church just wants money but then complain when the church doesn't have enough money to help everyone."

"That makes sense"

"That's just the short version of our months and months of talking. Sorry, I did not call to preach."

"You're good. You wanted to ask me something?"

"Yes". "Your dad wants to know if its okay for him to share his testimony."

"Don't you have to be a Christian first?" I laughed a little.

"Oh, sorry, I should have led with that. He became a Christian last night. He wants to share his testimony. With the whole church. He wanted to make sure it was okay with you. I told him it was fine with me."

If I were into the dramatics, I would have dropped the phone.

I drove to dad's house the next day by myself. He was already expecting me when I pulled up. He was finishing a cigarette and put it out when he saw me.

He kept a bottle of really nice lavender hand sanitizer by the door so he could keep the smell off his hands.

He really was trying.

"So I guess you've got news for me?" I asked. Thinking to what the pastor said about him giving his life to Jesus last night. I was walking up to him when I said it so he didn't hear me very well.

He repeated what he thought I said. "You've heard from the News? I didn't think they'd contact you today," he said.

"Huh?" I got on the porch. "The News is contacting me?

Why?"

"Oh I thought that's what you said. A while ago one of those reporters was at my sentencing and gave me his card. He said if I ever wanted to do an interview to let him know. I actually threw it away- in my very own trash can when I cleaned out my pockets. I sure as... (He stopped. Watching his language was really hard for him), I sure didn't want to talk to no reporter."

We went inside his trailer and he continued. "So, you know I'd been talking to that preacher and I started thinking about things and maybe I needed to change my life. I mean, doing it my way wasn't working very well. So yesterday I called him up and said "alright, I'm doing it. Walk me through it."

Dad told me he prayed with the preacher what Christians call "the sinner's prayer". Easy as A - B -C.

He Admitted he was a sinner.

He Believed that Jesus died to take his place in hell. He believed he rose from the dead.

And he was Committed to a life of serving God and following Jesus.

"I finished the prayer and I felt good. I finally felt clean. My daughter knew my old evil self and brought me to justice. The judge knew what I had done and handed down my punishment. Jesus and God knew what I was and I was still forgiven. I don't think I can ever repay what I've done. Not to you, to your mom or society. I learned from the pastor that what I've been given is grace and mercy. Mercy is what the judge gave me. I deserved a harsh punishment but I was given counseling, which was mercy. After all I have done to you and even before my day in court, you'd bring me food and check on me. That was grace.

I thought that if someone as horrible as me could feel this

free and was given mercy and grace, then maybe someone like me needs to hear my story. Maybe I shouldn't keep it to myself."

He took a breath. "So I thought about that reporter and I thought about what you said about your prayer. How you gave your decision to God and to make it easy or something."
I nodded.
"Well, I only prayed like once in my life and all I did was repeat the pastor and it was an ABC prayer so I'm not really good at it but I tried anyway. Stacey this is so crazy! I prayed something like 'God, if you want me to tell my story to that reporter, have him find me again. Amen. 'And that was it. I didn't feel anything like a *mighty wind* or anything. But I still felt clean. Hell, I had prayed twice in one night."
I smiled when he said "sorry. I mean, heck."
"So cleaned up the house and took out the trash and that little *bas*...(he stopped again) *that* reporter's card was stuck to the bottom of the dang trash bag! I must have stared at that card for 5 minutes. I know it was an answer to my prayers but I just couldn't believe it. I guess God wanted me to talk to him. It was gross and the card was soaked with something but I called his number. It was like 10 at night and he answered. He's going to do an interview with us and then come to hear my testimony on Sunday. Not this Sunday, the next one. He's got to cover a golf tournament."
I sat there smiling, laughing, and shaking my head in disbelief.

He told his story to a packed house. Word got out that Robert McClain was a Christian and he was going to be in a church telling his story.
The reporter's story ran in the paper and the local news

even aired some of his hearing. The segment was called "Forgiveness, a Redemption Story". My dad got up and was really honest. *Uncomfortably honest.* There were a lot of people there who had never been to church but came just to hear this guy talk. So many people really related to dad and his upbringing. I'm sure you can find his testimony somewhere online but if you understand that *hurt* people, hurt people and abused people, *abuse* people, then my father's story is one of a million. But there's only one Jesus. My dad said it best and simple. "You've tried it your way. Now try this. What do you have to lose?"
He had lost everything and he got it all back plus more.
He got a standing ovation. Me, Cash and the Rae clan were in the front row for support but he didn't need us. My dad did amazing. So many people came up to ask him questions and even more called him later to talk in private. Dad always told them to confess to law enforcement and God but not to leave either one out.
Dad called me and told me that several other preachers have asked that he come to their churches to speak and he even got a call from a public school superintendent to talk! They said he could share his faith as part of his story, as long as the focus wasn't about religion. "That's fine", dad told me. "I hate religion. I don't have one.
 I have a relationship with Jesus. I'll sneak that in."
My dad loved to get over on somebody.

Back to dating life and Cash.
Where did I leave off, oh yes.
Cash said to me one day sitting in the stands at a Bull Dogs game,
"I've been thinking about you a lot, your parents, your life, your faith. If you had been raised by the father you have now, your life would have been so much happier. I want

what you have. I want what your dad has."
No one had ever said those words before!
"I want to become a Christian, . I really like you and I guess I need to start with the truth."
He handed me a familiar Bull Dog keychain.
I laughed. He was giving me his keychain? But didn't quite get the joke. "Stacey, they were *my* keys, to my locker at the station. I didn't know how to go after you when we first met. I knew they weren't yours. But they are now, Keys to my heart and all the stuff that's in my locker. I think its gym socks. But it's all yours"

I smiled. With teeth.

Made in the USA
Columbia, SC
08 May 2024